BEWARE AND STOGIE

JESSIE HAAS

BEWARE AND STOGIE

with pictures by the author

GREENWILLOW BOOKS  NEW YORK

Library of Congress Cataloging-in-Publication Data

Haas, Jessie.
Beware and Stogie / by Jessie Haas ;
with illustrations by the author.
p.   cm.
Summary: When Stogie, Gramp's untamed horse,
escapes during a storm, Lily and her horse Beware are
the ones who bring Stogie home again.
ISBN 0-688-15605-3
[1. Horses—Fiction.   2. Grandfathers—Fiction.
3. Ranch life—Fiction.]   I. Title.
PZ7.H1129Bdf   1998   [Fic]—dc21
97-33035   CIP   AC

FOR PAT SAGER,
in memory of Par

BEWARE AND STOGIE

CHAPTER ONE

"I'M SCARED," MOM SAYS, from the doorway of Lily's room. "Can I get in with you?"

"Yes," Lily says. She moves over in bed and sits hugging her knees. Mom slides under the sheet, but she doesn't lie down. She and Lily look out the black window at the black sky.

"Wind," Mom says. "I don't know—sometimes it's even worse than lightning."

"I know," says Lily. Lightning comes quickly and then goes away. This wind just keeps on roaring. A leftover hurricane came through two days ago. After the rain the air stayed smothery and hot. Now cold air from Canada is pushing the hurricane air away. It breaks off tree branches, and rattles windows, and bangs into the sides of the house.

The black night makes Lily feel blind. She reaches over and pushes the switch on the bedside lamp. The switch clicks, but nothing happens.

"The electricity's out," Mom says.

Lily reaches for Mom's hand. "I hope Beware is okay." Beware is out there in the wind and dark.

"She'll be fine," Mom says. "The wind can't hurt a horse."

"It can't hurt us either," Lily says, and Mom laughs.

"Look," she says. A huge black cloud sails across the black sky. The rim of the cloud is silver with moonlight.

"It's clearing up," Mom says. "We'll have a beautiful day tomorrow."

Lily watches the ribbon of silver twist along the

edge of the cloud. The cloud sails swiftly past the window, and another pushes behind it. The long roar of the wind dies down for a moment.

Then from far away, from down near the horse pasture, comes a sound like gunshots. *Pop*-pop-pop-pop-pop!

Lily and Mom squeeze hands. There's a long, loud raking sound, the sound of something breaking, and then a crash.

"A tree," Mom says. "A big tree must have fallen."

Lily doesn't say anything. She knows how Mom will answer. But she wonders, is Beware all right?

Someone walks out of the downstairs bedroom. The kitchen door opens. After a minute Lily calls, "Gramp?"

He answers her from out on the porch. "Tree down somewhere."

"We heard," Mom says.

"Horses are running," Gramp says. "Hope my fence is still up."

"Should we go see?" Lily is already halfway out of bed, feeling in the dark for her clothes.

"Don't bother!" Gramp says. "The batteries are gone in this dadblamed flashlight! Wouldn't you just know it?" Lily hears him grunt, and then she hears the flashlight thud on the lawn. "We'll have to wait till daylight."

"Lie down, Lily," Mom says. Lily does, but she stays awake a long time, trying to hear the hoofbeats.

When Lily wakes up, Mom is getting out of bed. Downstairs the kitchen door bangs shut. The early-morning sky is baby blue, and a small white cloud stands still outside Lily's window. Lily remembers the black and silver clouds last night, and she gets up quickly.

Already Gran is at the kitchen stove, and the phone is ringing. Mom answers it, and she tells Gran, "They want him on the road crew. A lot of trees came down last night."

"I doubt they'll get him," Gran says as Lily goes out the door.

From the front step she can see all the way across the pasture. Gramp looks small down there, trudging up the slope toward the far fence. A silver green heap of leaves and branches lies across the fence line: one of the big maples.

Lily looks along the fence of Beware's pasture. She's looking so hard for broken places that at first she doesn't see Beware and the pony. They're grazing peacefully in the middle of their field.

But where are the other horses? The Girls, Gramp's big blond workhorses, should be following him up the hill. The bunch of horses he bought last week to sell again should be there. Stogie, the black Morgan that no one can catch, should be galloping and snorting and looking dangerous.

There are no horses anywhere, and the cow and calf are gone, too. Gramp is all alone in the big pasture. Lily sees him climb over the fallen branches and bend down outside the fence. He must be looking at tracks. Now he stands up and looks off toward the woods and then the other way, toward the swamp. After a minute he turns back. Lily picks the flashlight up off the lawn and goes down to meet him.

"Morning," Gramp says, and reaches into his pocket for his pipe. He bites onto the stem. Then he takes the pipe out of his mouth and says, "They split up. We've got the day's work cut out for us."

"The road crew wants you," Lily says.

"They aren't gettin' me!" says Gramp. "If that cow or that team gets onto a road and somebody hits 'em—" He doesn't say any more.

Lily looks toward the road that passes in front of the house. It runs downhill to a bigger road. Off in the hills behind the pasture are other roads: logging trails, dirt roads, and a mile away, another wide paved road.

"We should hurry," she says.

"Breakfast first," says Gramp. "This is going to be a big job." In the kitchen he takes the cup of coffee Gran hands him and goes to the phone.

"Sorry, Ron, can't help you out today," he says. "I've got critters loose all over kingdom come."

He's quiet for a minute. Then his eyes start to bulge, and his nose gets red. "You let a car hit that work team at fifty miles an hour, Ron, and you'll know you've got troubles!" he says, and he hangs up the phone with a crash. *"Idiot!"*

"The world isn't built around farmers anymore, Linwood," Gran says. "Sit down and eat your breakfast."

Gramp sits, and he does eat. But he hardly seems to notice the crisp hash browns or the eggs. He's looking off into space, and Lily knows what he sees. The red-and-white cow and the calf with her long white stockings. The Girls, turning their big heads and blinking their blond eyelashes. Beautiful Stogie, with his wild, matted mane. They are running loose, and anything could happen.

"At least Beware's still here," Lily says.

"Yes, Lily, I'm glad," says Gramp.

"No, I mean, I can ride her out to find the others. She can help."

Gramp looks across the table at Lily, and he smiles for the first time this morning. "You're right. She can."

CHAPTER TWO

"LINWOOD!" GRAN SAYS. Gramp looks at her, and she looks hard back at him. She is trying to tell him something without using words, but Gramp doesn't get it.

"What?" he asks.

"What happens if she finds them?" Gran asks. "Out in the middle of that bunch, all fighting and kicking! What happens if she catches up with that Stogie?"

Oh! Lily didn't think about it before, but those

horses are new to one another. Gramp just bought them. All week they've been biting and chasing and squealing out in the pasture, working out which one is boss. Only the Girls and Stogie always live here, and Stogie is boss. But he has to teach that all over again to each new bunch of horses.

The new horses don't know Beware. They will want to see if they can boss her, and they won't notice Lily on her back.

Gramp keeps looking at Gran. After a minute he shakes his head. "It pains me," he says, "but you're right. Lily, you and Beware can go after the cow and calf. They went off into the swamp, and the horses went the other way. That suit you, Gracie?"

"And if you're wrong?" Gran asks. "What does she do if she does come up on the crowd of them?"

"She gets off before they get close," Gramp says, "and she takes the bridle off, so Beware doesn't step on the reins, and she walks home and tells me where they are. She's a smart girl, Gracie. She knows how to handle herself."

But a few minutes later, down at the barn, Gramp says, "Isn't often your grandma gets the jump on me like that. If you see those horses, Lily, you get off right away. Don't wait for 'em to come up to you. And don't worry about Beware. They won't hurt her."

"I know," Lily says. She's seen the horses fight. They squeal as loud as elephants and strike the air with their front hooves. They kick and chase. They never seem to hurt one another, but Lily wouldn't want to be mixed up in it.

Beware waits at the gate for her breakfast. Even after the wild night she is calm and well mannered. But her eyes shine as if she remembers the excitement, and on the way to the barn she stops once. She looks off into the big pasture. After a minute she sighs.

"I know, girl," Lily says. "Where did they go?"

She feeds Beware and brushes her and gives her a cough drop. Beware crunches it down. Cough drops are her favorite treat. Lily slips another one in her pocket for later.

While she is saddling, Gramp comes up with his

long black whip. "This might help you drive the old cow," he says. "And if that bunch of horses comes up on you, you can use it to hold 'em off." Lily has seen Gramp do that when he walks into a bunch of horses. He doesn't hit them. He just holds the whip out, and the horses leave a space around him.

Mom comes in. Gramp hands her two halters, two ropes, and a coffee can full of grain. He slings more halters over his shoulder, picks up his pail of fencing equipment, and looks at his watch. He makes a face. "We're off like a herd of turtles!"

Lily feels tall, riding across the big pasture beside Mom and Gramp. Beware turns her head from side to side. Lily can see her nostrils flare as she sniffs the cool, crisp air.

When she sees the fallen tree, Beware stops in her tracks. She blows her breath out in light, rattling snorts. What is it?

Lily waits. After a minute Beware takes a step,

and another. She's still crouched, though, ready to jump if anything moves.

Then suddenly Beware relaxes. She walks right up and sniffs the leaves. She tears off a mouthful and starts to crunch. "I always wonder if they feel embarrassed," Mom says, "when they've been spooked by something perfectly normal."

Lily doesn't think the fallen tree is perfectly normal. It looks bigger on its side than it did standing up. The heap of leaves and branches is as high as Lily's head, even now when she's sitting on Beware. The trunk stands naked behind the fence. Only one small leafy branch is left on it. Spikes of wood stab up toward the sky.

Gramp snips the barbed wire and pulls it to one side. "Hope nobody got cut," he says, and he looks on every strand of wire for blood or hair. He doesn't find any.

"All right, Lily, go ahead," he says. Lily rides through the opening in the fence.

On the other side the muddy ground is trampled.

The dinner-plate tracks the Girls make are big enough that Lily can see the calf's prints crossing them, small and split like a deer's track. The cow's hooves have made long, slidy Vs in the mud, across the hayfield toward the swamp.

The smaller horse tracks are all mixed together. There are perfect horseshoe prints, with every nail showing. There are long slides and smears. Big chunks of turf have been torn and turned upside down.

On top of all the other tracks are the ragged, rough-edged marks of Stogie's hooves. No one can catch Stogie, so no one has trimmed his feet. His hooves grow long and break off on their own.

"See, Barb?" Gramp says, pointing uphill with his chin. "They went that way, and that black son of a gun was chasing them."

"What will you do when you find them?" Lily asks. Mom and Gramp have grain, and the horses will want it. They'll crowd and push and kick at one another, with Mom and Gramp in the middle.

"We'll be all right," Gramp says. "Got a lifetime

supply of horsewhips right here." He nods at the heap of maple branches. "So go on and see if you can find that cow. If she'll drive, drive her back here. If she won't, at least you can tell me where she is."

Lily turns Beware along the row of cow tracks and starts toward the swamp.

Mom calls after her, "Be careful!"

Chapter Three

ALL BY HERSELF Lily rides across the hayfield. The morning sun is hot on her cheek. It makes bright curves along the top of Beware's neck and sparkles on the wet grass. Lily can hear Gramp's hammer ringing on the fence post. She tries to listen past it for the sound of hoofbeats. But the only hooves she hears are Beware's.

At the swamp's edge a red-winged blackbird cries *check! check!* from high in a poplar tree. Lily stops Beware where the land dips down. She looks carefully at the ground ahead. She doesn't want to ride Beware through deep mud or water.

The cow's tracks make a dotted line through the grass. Under the grass the ground is very wet. The tracks are big and muddy. Farther ahead the tracks look smaller and lighter-colored. The ground is drier there.

"Easy," Lily says to Beware. She shortens the reins, and she squeezes softly with her legs. "Walk."

Beware slides down the slope and lurches as she hits the mud. She tosses her nose, pulling the reins through Lily's hands.

"Hey!" Lily says. Beware isn't supposed to pull like that. But Beware doesn't try to go faster. She just puts her head down to watch the footing. Her hooves make loud squelches going into the mud and loud sucking noises coming out. Mud splats on Lily's cheek.

Then Beware's back rises up, and she scrambles onto drier land. Her breath comes in big puffs. "Whoa," Lily says. "Good girl!" Beware was bossy, pulling the reins like that, but she disobeyed only so she could do her job better.

Beware rests for a moment. Lily leaves the reins long and loose and lets Beware decide when she's ready to go on.

When Beware does start, she seems to know that she's supposed to follow the cow's tracks. She walks along quickly, with her nose close to the ground. Lily leans to one side so she can see the tracks, too.

All at once Beware stops and snorts. Lily grabs at Beware's neck to keep from tipping forward. "What's the matter? I don't see anything."

Beware doesn't seem to see anything either. She's looking into the grass, but not at any one spot. "Is it a snake?" Lily isn't afraid of snakes, way up here on Beware's back. "Come on, walk!"

Beware takes another step. Lily hears the black-bird, loud and close.

Suddenly a lot of little brown birds are in the air, flying just above the tops of the grass stems. They flutter in front of Beware and disappear into the grass on the other side of the cow's trail. *Check!* the black-bird calls, swooping to a lower branch.

"We won't hurt them," Lily tells him, and she makes Beware trot on quickly. Red-winged blackbirds sometimes dive-bomb people to protect their babies.

For a second the cow's tracks disappear, and then Lily sees them up ahead, making a dotted line straight toward the middle of the swamp. Why did the cow come in here? Lily wonders. Where did she think she was going?

Beware puts her ears back and shakes her head. A big deerfly, like a yellow-brown arrowhead, is biting her neck. Lily squashes it. Blood stains her fingers. Then something like a hot needle stabs into the back of her arm.

"*Ow!*" She slaps at it, but that fly gets away. "I hope you bit that stupid cow, too!" Lily says.

Here in the swamp some of the hot hurricane air still lingers. The sun draws up dampness from the ground. The air is hazy, and mosquitoes swirl and whine. They land on Beware, but when they smell fly spray, they rise and land on Lily instead. Lily holds the reins in one hand and slaps with the other. The morning seems long, and the swamp seems big and empty.

An airplane makes a white trail overhead. After a while Lily can hear the sound it makes. Far away a truck growls along the road, and a horn beeps. Somewhere between the road and the swamp, or on the dark pine-covered hill, the horses and the cow are running free. But it doesn't seem possible they can be near. Nothing is near, except woodpeckers, and mosquitoes, and frogs. . . .

Beware stops.

"What?" Lily looks at the ground. It seems almost dry here, but horses can sense things people can't. Maybe beneath the dry-looking surface the mud is deep, like quicksand.

But the cow's tracks go straight across it, with the calf's tracks scampering alongside. Lily follows with her eyes. The tracks curve away, into a brushy thicket.

That's where Beware is looking, too. She bobs her head, the way horses do when they can't quite tell what they're seeing.

In the thicket something moves.

Stogie! Lily jerks the reins without meaning to. She clutches the whip. She can picture Stogie hiding there, his ears flat back, his strong yellow teeth ready to bite. His long mane hangs like ropes. His ragged hooves paw the ground.

But Beware steps lightly forward with her neck arched. That's the way she steps when she sees a deer and wants to follow it. Lily's heart beats hard. She should get off—

And then she is close enough to see, and it is the cow, standing in a cloud of mosquitoes with the calf at her feet.

CHAPTER FOUR

THE COW SHAKES HER EARS and slings her head at the flies. Sunlight glistens on her broad pink muzzle. She blinks her white eyelashes at Lily and Beware. Then she nudges the calf.

The calf gets up slowly. She stretches, arching her back and curling her tail. Then she reaches under her mother's belly and begins to nurse. The cow stares at Lily.

Now what? Lily wonders. If she rides Beware close, she'll drive the cow deeper into the swamp. If they stay where they are, they will block her from going back the way she came.

"We need to get behind her," Lily tells Beware. She rides off the path, looking for a safe way to get around the cow.

The minute Beware moves out of the way, the cow gives a low bawl. She trots back along her own path. The calf trots behind, and Beware follows, without Lily having to urge her.

The cow goes fast. She disappears behind bushes and tall stands of grass. The calf skitters after. Beware trots hard to keep up, but she doesn't have to do any herding. The cow leads her calf straight back the way she came, toward home.

"Then why did you come *in* here?" Lily yells after them. She is hot, and her bug bites itch. She thought it would be fun to herd the cow. She thought it would be interesting. It isn't interesting to scramble back through the swamp, getting spattered with mud from Beware's hooves and *still* being bitten. "You stupid cow!" Lily yells.

The little brown birds flutter up from the grass. *Check!* their father cries, and swoops down. He's too late for the cow, too late for the calf, but Lily feels the breeze from his wings on her face. She ducks and makes Beware go faster. The ground beneath them squelches and sucks. Then with a grunt Beware heaves up the bank. She pauses, breathing hard. Across the field Lily sees the cow and calf galloping. Their tails kink in the air. They head straight for the fallen tree.

But Gramp put the wire back! They can't get in!

The cow doesn't pause. Lily hears a *skreek!* of wire, and then the cow is inside the pasture. The calf skims along beside her.

Check! The blackbird dives.

"Trot, Beware!"

Gramp stapled two strands of barbed wire right into the fallen tree trunk. They are still up, and Lily doesn't see how the cow could fit between them. But a tuft of red hair is caught in the top strand, and a tuft of white belly hair is caught in the bottom strand, and there is the cow in the middle of the pasture. She must have pushed the wires up and down, and if it hurt a little, she didn't care.

The cow looks back at Lily and Beware. Her head is high, and her eyes are narrow. Lily makes a face at her. She tries to turn Beware toward the barn.

But Beware is gazing into the pasture. Lily looks where Beware's ears point. There in the shade are the Girls, scratching each other's backs. All around them are the other horses, dozing and grazing and swishing flies.

"Oh," Lily says. "That was easy!"

At the barn she unsaddles Beware, and walks her cool, and puts her in a stall with water and a little grain.

Then Lily walks up to the house. Sunlight flashes off the windshields of Gramp's truck and Mom's car. Good! They're still here. Lily can tell them how she caught the cow.

But Gran is alone. The kitchen is full of steam and the smell of cooked tomatoes. The pressure cooker rattles on the stove.

"Where are Mom and Gramp?" Lily asks.

Gran turns from the sink. "I have no idea."

"Well, did they have trouble with the horses?"

"They didn't catch the horses," Gran says. She slips the boiled skin off a big tomato. "I did."

"You did! *How?"* Gran never touches a horse if she can help it. She doesn't like horses.

"Easiest thing in the world," Gran says. Her voice is sharp, but Lily sees her cheek dent as she holds in a smile. "Half an hour after you all left, I looked out the window, and there they were. I just opened the gate and let them in."

"Oh, poor Gramp!" Lily says. "Poor Mom! It's too bad we can't tell them."

"I did beep the truck horn," Gran says, "but no one heard."

Lily remembers hearing the horn. It sounded as if it were out on the road.

"It's just as well they didn't come," Gran says after a minute. "That Stogie didn't come back with the rest. He's still out there."

Lily has a big glass of milk and a sandwich. She helps Gran with the tomatoes. Then she sits on the porch and watches until Mom and Gramp come out of the woods.

She sees Gramp stop, take off his floppy green hat, and rub the top of his head. He says something to Mom, and his glasses flash as he laughs.

Then he looks harder. He walks over to the fence. The Girls come to him, and he strokes their noses. But he looks past at the other horses. Mom looks, too, and they both shake their heads. They walk slowly up the hill.

"Came back on their own, didn't they?" Gramp says when he comes in. "Gracie, you win again!"

"Lily got the cow," Gran says.

"All we got is tired," says Mom, sitting down at

the table. "You'd think it would be easy to track nine horses, wouldn't you? But the tracks just disappeared under the pines."

"Like Stogie," Lily says.

Gramp stands frowning out the window. "Something must have happened to him."

"Maybe he just ran off," Gran says. "A wild animal like that—"

"That horse is no wilder than I am!" Gramp says. "I saw him ridden the day I bought him. He's just smart, and the feller I bought him from was pretty smart, too! No, Gracie, horses like to be with other horses. He'd stay with the bunch if he could."

"Maybe he's broken into somebody's pasture," Mom says.

"Then why didn't the rest of 'em?"

"If he got separated from the others . . . if he got lost . . ." Lily can tell that Mom doesn't believe that happened. Not really.

Gramp scratches his cheek. He didn't take time to shave this morning, and Lily can hear his bristles rasp. His eyes look far away, the way they do when he thinks about Stogie. Gramp has always wanted a good Morgan, since he was a little boy. He wanted to take Stogie to the show at Tunbridge and pull logs with him, drive him in races, and have Mom or Lily ride him. He has spent the past two years watching Stogie graze in the summer, tossing him hay in the winter, and trying to catch him. Now just seeing Stogie would be enough, just knowing where he is.

"Well," Gramp says finally, "guess I'd better call the sheriff."

He goes to the telephone. "Hi, Ken. Woody Griffin here. Got a black horse loose somewhere in this county. . . . Yup, he's got a halter on, but the fact is, I can't catch the son of a gun when he's in my own pasture, so I don't have much hope of catchin' him now." The sheriff says something. Lily sees Gramp hesitate. Then he says, "Yes, Ken, if he's making trouble, you've got my permission to shoot him."

CHAPTER FIVE

LILY AND MOM LOOK AT each other across the table. Gramp loves Stogie. He's ashamed that he bought a horse nobody can catch. He knows that Stogie is useless. But he's beautiful, too. Gramp likes having him out there, looking so wild.

"They shouldn't *shoot* him," Lily says when Gramp comes back from the phone. "He's afraid of people, really."

"I know, Lily," Gramp says. "But if he gets in with somebody's horses or into their garden, what are we going to do? He could hurt people just trying to get away."

Lily knows Gramp is right. She can see Stogie's big black body crashing fences, shoving and shouldering people. She can see him kicking dogs and frightening children. Lily isn't afraid of horses the way some people are. That's because she knows how to tell them what to do. But no one can tell Stogie things because he won't let people close. Maybe he doesn't even remember the way people and horses talk to one another.

"But couldn't we *look?*"

"Lily," Gran says. She puts a sandwich in front of Gramp, and she opens him a bottle of homemade root beer.

"I've looked," Gramp says. "I'll keep on lookin'. But he could be anywhere, Lily. For all I know he's out on that hillside hurt, and we walked right by him."

Lily has never thought about Stogie being hurt. Stogie is fast and surefooted. His black legs are round and smooth, like iron bars.

"Maybe he's caught in wire," Mom says. She gets up suddenly. "I have to go to work now, but I'll try to get out early."

"I'll go drive around a little," Gramp says. "Maybe I'll see him."

In a minute they both are gone. "He hardly tasted this root beer!" Gran says.

Lily turns from the kitchen window. She and Gran look at each other. After a minute Gran sighs. She looks at the crumbs she is sweeping off the table.

"I was brought up to take care of the animals before I took care of myself," she says. The corners of her mouth turn down.

Lily waits.

"*Is* that horse afraid of people?" Gran asks.

"Yes," Lily says. She doesn't know how afraid Stogie is. She knows that a frightened horse is a dangerous horse. But she says, "The only thing he wants is not to be caught."

Gran pours the root beer into two small glasses.

She gives one to Lily, and she takes a sip from the other. "There's never been a more useless animal on this place," she says after a moment. "But if he's out there somewhere, suffering . . ."

It feels to Lily as if they are two grown-ups talking. Something serious has happened, and each of them must decide what to do.

Gran is waiting, and now Lily knows what to say. "I thought I'd ride up on the hill and look for him."

Gran nods. Her eyes are wide and steady, and they meet Lily's eyes straight on. "I know you'll be very, very careful," she says.

Lily rides Beware up Gramp's wood road. The air is cool under the trees. High above, the leaves shift, and bright blue sky shows through. This is one of Lily's favorite places to ride, but today she lets only a little part of herself enjoy the air and blue sky. The rest of her listens for Stogie, and watches the ground, and stays prepared. That is what Gran depends on her to do.

Beware trots strongly. The snap of the lead rope around Lily's waist clicks in time to Beware's steps. Nobody can catch Stogie, so nobody can lead him, but Lily brought a rope anyway. She brought the whip, too.

Partway up the hill Lily gets off to look for horse tracks. She bends close to the ground. Beware looks, too. She noses the dirt, and then she nudges Lily's hand. Maybe Lily has found something. Maybe it's good to eat.

"No, silly! I'm looking for tracks."

There are no tracks. There are no sounds, except a blue jay calling. It's so quiet nothing as big as a horse could be nearby.

But the cow was there, Lily remembers. It was just as quiet out in the swamp, and the cow was right there.

Lily rides on. She listens, but she can hear only

the soft thud of Beware's hooves. If Stogie were near, Beware could smell him. She could hear him, better than Lily could. But Beware doesn't seem to sense anything. Her ears point gently up the road.

Where Gramp has cut wood there is more sky and more sunlight. Ferns grow in the bright shade between the stumps, and Beware keeps reaching down to snatch a bite. "Hey!" Lily says. "We aren't on a picnic!"

She rides around the edge of the cleared spot. No tracks. No tracks. No tracks—wait! Here the ferns are bruised and broken. Clods of dirt are kicked up, and there are tracks, a big braid of them.

Lily dismounts. She holds the reins loosely and lets Beware eat ferns while she studies the ground. She finds Stogie's track, notched and ragged, on top of all the others. When they came through here, Stogie was still chasing them.

Lily sits back on her heels. She tries to put herself inside Stogie's mind and understand what he wants.

Stogie thinks he is a wild horse. He acts like the

boss of a herd. Once he got his herd out of the pasture, where would he want to take them?

Away. Across the mountain.

Lily looks toward the uphill side of the clearing and up, and up, to where the edge of the mountain meets the sky. That's where Stogie would go.

Lily can see him in her mind's eye, weaving back and forth behind the others. The Girls want to go home. They keep looking back. But Stogie bites them. He throws himself at them like a black spear, and he drives them uphill. The Girls are big and slow. They can't outrun Stogie. How did they get away to lead the others home?

Something happened to Stogie. That's the only way it could have happened. Lily can see it different ways in her mind. Stogie steps in a hole and breaks his leg. He gets caught in wire. A bear comes out of the woods, and Stogie turns to protect his herd—

The reins pull in Lily's hand. She looks up. "*Hey!*" Beware has stepped on one of the reins. Before

Lily can move, Beware feels the pull. She tosses her head. The rein snaps.

"Oh, no!" Lily jumps up and catches Beware by the bridle. The rein is broken close to the bit ring. Beware rolls her eyes and snorts her breath out. It frightened her to feel herself suddenly caught like that.

"Stupid!" Lily tells herself. She should have watched Beware, not the horse herd in her head.

She tries to tie the broken rein around the bit ring. It makes a big knot that rubs the side of Beware's cheek. When Lily pulls the rein even a little bit, the knot comes untied.

Now what? Lily doesn't dare ride with only one rein. Even Beware isn't good enough for that. She'll have to walk back down the hill and see if she can find an old set of reins in the barn.

Or a lead rope. A lead rope would make a quick rein. . . .

And there's a lead rope right here, tied around Lily's waist.

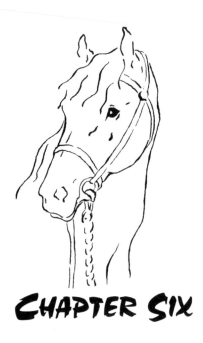

CHAPTER SIX

THE LEAD ROPE FEELS THICK in Lily's hand. She keeps lengthening it and shortening it, trying to make it feel right, as she rides along the edge of the clearing.

The tracks have disappeared over the bare ledge and the thick brown pine needles. Once Lily does see a narrow trail of bruised ferns, leading downhill. She finds a horse track there. It was made by a round, neat hoof that wore a horseshoe.

The sun turns some leaves gold and others deeper green. The breeze shifts them, and bright light slides along the ground. Up the hill Beware climbs, and then she picks her way down the other side. Together she and Lily decide which way to go. Sometimes Lily sees a mark on the ground that might be a track. Sometimes Beware moves forward with her ears pricked, finding an opening among the trees that looks like a path.

But it never is a track, and there never is a path. Lily goes a long way, down and down again, until she can hear the cars on the big road.

Near the road the ground gets rough. The trees grow small and close together. Lily turns Beware around, and they pick their way back to the top of the hill.

Lily stops there to let Beware catch her breath. The hill spreads down behind her and in front of her. It drops into deep folds. Brooks and small dirt roads are hidden there. Other hills rise up beyond. They are covered with trees, and they are all quiet.

"Maybe we'll go home," Lily says. "Maybe Stogie's found his way back." She knows it won't be true. But the hills are too big to find a horse in.

"We'll go home a different way," she tells Beware. "If we can find it." There's a trail that leads down the shoulder of the hill. Mom cleared it years ago, and Lily cleared it again this spring. But the trail is steep and narrow, so Lily doesn't take it often. It begins somewhere here, where Gramp has been cutting trees.

Lily angles across the cleared slope. There was a hemlock, and the trail started behind it. That hemlock is gone now. There are new stumps, and new brush piles, and new growths of ferns. . . .

Beware bobs her nose, asking Lily for more rein. Her ears point gently forward, and she steps eagerly. Beware seems to know exactly where she's going. She crosses the bare, confusing slope, and suddenly there is the trail, slicing down between the thick-growing saplings.

The trail is a green tunnel. The light is dim, like the light at the bottom of the sea. Lily can see the gray stubs of branches that Mom cut long ago and fresher brown stubs of branches that she'd cut herself.

There are other branches she should have cut. They arch across the path, and Lily has to keep ducking. Once she doesn't duck far enough, and a branch smacks hard on her helmet. Once Beware swerves and bangs Lily's knee into a tree trunk.

"*Ow!* Beware, slow down!" Lily leans back in the saddle. She thinks about keeping her legs against Beware's sides. She thinks about keeping her rump down in the saddle. Riding right, the way she would ride in a show ring, helps her stop Beware from going too fast.

It feels good to ride this way. Lily is thinking about that when suddenly Beware stops.

"What?"

Beware stares down the narrow path. She blows her breath out hard.

The path ahead is dark and dim. Lily stares into the darkness, trying to see what Beware sees.

The darkness moves.

Whoosh! goes Beware's breath, and she's going backward, fast. Lily can hardly tell what's happening. "Whoa!" she says, but Beware keeps backing until she bumps into a tree.

Then she stands still. Her neck is high and hard like a rock. Her ears strain forward, and the breath in her nostrils goes *p-r-r! P-r-r-r!*

"Easy," Lily whispers. She has never seen Beware this frightened before. Is it a moose down there? A bear? There's nowhere to run except straight uphill, and Lily knows that a bear can run faster than a horse uphill. But the trees grow close together here. Beware couldn't push between them.

There's a sound. To Lily it seems like a growl. But Beware snorts and bobs her head, as if she is suddenly less afraid.

The sound comes again. Beware flicks one ear back at Lily, almost as if she wonders what Lily thinks. Then she takes a step forward.

Lily grabs the saddle. Beware wouldn't go toward a bear, would she?

Beware takes two steps. She stops, she snorts, she listens, and she steps again. Lily just hangs on to the front of the saddle. If Beware decides to turn and run, Lily wants to stay on top of her.

The darkness groans and moves again. Now Lily can see a long black tail, hanging in ropes.

Stogie.

He is facing downhill, and he's on his feet. His head is high. Why doesn't he turn? He isn't even looking at Lily and Beware. What is wrong with him? Doesn't he know they're here?

Lily shifts the whip into her free hand, so she can use it if she needs to. She shortens the real rein and the lead rope rein, so she'll be able to control Beware.

"Hey!" she yells.

Stogie's tail swishes limply. High against the leaves, Lily sees the white of his eye. But he doesn't move.

CHAPTER SEVEN

LILY CAN'T THINK WHAT TO DO.

She could yell at Stogie and try to make him move. But if he's hurt, moving might hurt him even more.

She could ride up closer and try to see what's the matter. Will he turn then and bite Beware?

She could tie Beware to a tree and *walk* up to Stogie. Beware is wearing her bridle, though, and it isn't right to tie a horse by the bridle. If Beware pulled back, the bit could hurt her mouth.

Stogie shifts his back legs. Lily hears his breath rattle in and groan out.

"All right!" Lily gets off Beware. She unsnaps the lead rope from the bit, and she snaps it into the narrow leather strap of Beware's noseband. Then she ties the lead rope rein around a small sapling. Now if Beware pulls back, she won't be pulling against the bit. She'll probably break the bridle, but she won't hurt herself.

"You stand, Beware!" Lily says. She grips the whip tightly, and she walks toward Stogie.

"Whoa, boy," she says. "Easy." Stogie's hindquarters fill the path. Lily doesn't want to get close enough to be kicked.

The saplings beside the trail grow close together like a wall. A horse couldn't fit between them, but Lily can, just barely. She turns herself sideways. She squeezes between trees and bends branches and pushes little saplings down until she is right up beside Stogie's shoulders. Only a thin screen of saplings comes between them, like the bars on a jailhouse window.

Still Stogie doesn't move. Lily looks at his ragged feet and his strong, round legs. They seem perfectly normal.

She looks at his broad chest and his arching neck. His hair sticks out in little spikes, as if he has been sweating. But Lily can't see anything wrong.

She looks at his head. His eye rolls to look back at her. The white of his eye is bloodshot. His old leather halter is twisted on his head, so the side strap is right up under his eye. Lily can see something dark beneath his jaw.

Beware snorts, and Stogie groans back at her. He shifts his legs, but his head stays perfectly still. Lily pokes her head out between the last row of saplings.

"Oh, *I* see!" The dark thing under Stogie's jaw is a branch, one that Lily trimmed this summer, a strong, springy branch. The jaw strap of Stogie's halter is twisted tight around it. That's what is holding him still. He can't break the branch off the tree, and he can't pull loose from it.

"Stogie, you wait!" Lily says. She pushes back

through the saplings and hurries to Beware. She'll ride up the trail to the clearing, and quickly down the wood road, and get Gramp. Gramp will cut the branch, and then Stogie will be free.

But when Lily turns Beware up the path, Stogie whinnies after her. He sounds breathless. Lily hears his feet crash in the dry sticks and leaves. She looks back.

Stogie is trying to twist around to see them. As Lily watches, his back feet slip on the path. They slide underneath his body, and then he is hanging from the branch. It bends with his weight, but it doesn't break.

Lily presses one hand to her mouth. There is nothing she can do. She watches Stogie thrash and flail and struggle until at last he finds his footing again.

He stands still on the path, the way he was when Lily found him. His breath is loud and harsh. His black sides heave. Lily can see the red of his nostrils and smell the hot new sweat that has broken out on his body. How long has Stogie been here? How many times has he slipped like that and struggled?

Stogie jerks his head against the halter and the branch. He's still trying to see Beware. "She's right here," Lily says. "I won't take her away." She rides down closer.

Now what *can* she do? Stogie must be freed soon. He's getting weak and tired. He could hang himself if he slipped again. He could get colic from having no water. He could go into shock.

Tie Beware here and run home? That will take a long time, and what if Beware gets loose? She would probably go home, and Stogie would go crazy.

Wait here? Gramp will come looking if Lily doesn't get back soon. But that could be a long time, too, and when he comes, he won't have a saw to cut the branch with.

If only Lily dared go right up to Stogie! Maybe she could get his halter off.

"What should I do?" she asks Beware. Beware blows softly through her nostrils. She can't answer

Lily the way a person would. All Beware wants is to go home.

Gramp would dare walk up to Stogie. Probably Mom would, too. Gran would tell them to be careful, but she would think they ought to do it.

What would she want Lily to do?

Stogie needs help. There is no one else to do it. Gran would want Lily to try—and be very, very careful.

Lily dismounts and ties Beware. She pushes back through the saplings. "Easy, Stogie," she says. "Easy." Her voice sounds scared to her. It sounds shaky. But when she gets to the last saplings, she pushes right through them and steps onto the path beside Stogie.

His black shoulder is hot, like the side of the wood stove. Lily can feel it without even touching him. There's foamy sweat on his neck where the branch has rubbed.

"Whoa, Stogie," Lily says. Stogie's bloodshot eye rolls. He shifts his front hooves. Lily has seen him strike with those hooves. They are as hard as hammers.

She knows she had better not get in front, where they could reach her.

She looks hard at the halter. The leather is old and stiff. The buckle is sunken down into the strap. With all that stiffness, and all Stogie's weight on it, that buckle will never come undone.

But high up next to Stogie's eye is the throat snap. If Lily can unclip that, the halter will slide right off over his head.

Can she reach it? Lily leans the whip against a tree, where she can get it quickly. She edges closer. "Easy," she says, and she puts her hand firmly on Stogie's shoulder.

Stogie's skin shudders. His breath rattles more quickly. Lily is the first person to touch him in two years. His ungroomed shoulder is hot beneath her hand, and Lily can feel that he is afraid of her.

All at once she loves Stogie. He's so big and dangerous and in so much trouble, and he is afraid of her.

"It's okay," she tells him. "It's okay, you silly

boy." She rubs her hand up his neck, making circles the way a mare does with her tongue as she licks her foal.

"There, does that hurt? You know, if you let people touch you, we could have taken this halter off a long time ago, and you wouldn't be in trouble now."

Lily stands on tiptoe. She can't quite reach. She's standing too far back, near Stogie's shoulder. To reach, she'll have to step in front of him.

"You could hurt me," she tells him. "But if you do, you won't get loose. Whoa now, Stogie. Stand." She steps right in front of Stogie's black, dangerous front feet. She reaches for the halter just as if he were Beware, and she unsnaps the snap.

The halter slides, all by itself. Stogie pulls back, and the branch springs up into the air with the old leather halter wrapped around it.

CHAPTER EIGHT

STOGIE IS FREE.

Lily is standing right in front of him. He could hurt her if he wanted. He could run away.

But Stogie just stands there. His head is down, level with his back. His ears go out to the sides, and he has worried wrinkles around his eyes. After a second he shakes himself.

That's good, Lily thinks. Horses shake themselves after rolling, or when the saddle is taken off, to settle back into their skins. It's a sign of good health.

But Stogie shakes carefully, as if it hurts, and then he hangs his head again.

"Poor guy!" Lily says. "How long were you stuck here?" A long time. The path under Stogie's feet is black and beaten with hoof marks. "Your neck must hurt," Lily says. "Let's get you home."

She pushes back through the saplings and trips on the fallen whip. When she bends to pick it up, she sees a huge horse track, the size of a dinner plate. "Oh!" The Girls came this way, and now Lily sees other tracks. All the horses must have come this way, and Stogie followed them, until his halter caught on the branch.

Beware wants to smell Lily's hands. She stops Lily from untying the lead rope, and she sniffs, sniffs, sniffs. All the while she gazes down the path at Stogie. Her eyes are wide and soft.

What is Beware thinking? What can she tell about Stogie by sniffing Lily's hands? Can she smell his fear? Can she smell his sore neck?

"Let's go," Lily says finally. The sun is behind

the hill now, and the shadows are long. Gran will be worried.

Stogie has started down the path. His steps seem loose and weak. Lily rides up behind him, not too close. She remembers now that she was supposed to get off Beware if Stogie was around. That way she wouldn't get caught in a horse fight.

But Stogie pays no attention to Beware. He just shambles down the path. Lily passes under the halter, hanging on the branch. She reaches up for it. It's still warm from Stogie's head. She slings it over her shoulder, and the snap clinks in time to Beware's steps.

Stogie shakes again. His matted mane flaps against his neck. Could anyone make Stogie's mane look nice? Lily doesn't think so. He'll have to be shaved—

"But nobody can catch him!" Lily says out loud. It's surprising to remember that, because she just touched Stogie. She just took his halter off, as if he were any other horse.

Now he is free again. He doesn't even have a halter on. What will Gramp think about that? Lily wonders.

Stogie's steps get quicker and stronger. He's walking the stiffness out of his legs. He dips and raises his neck, stretching the stiffness out of that, too.

"Feel better?" Lily asks.

Stogie stops. He cranes his neck and looks over his shoulder at Lily and Beware. His eye seems brighter now. He looks more like himself.

"Hey, walk on!" Lily says. She holds the whip up to show Stogie. He just looks at her. Then he groans. He stretches his neck down, and up, and starts walking again.

Soon he'll reach the bottom of the hill. The path crosses a brook there and widens out through a weedy meadow. When he gets there, Stogie will have plenty of room to turn and sniff Beware. Then the squealing and striking will begin. Before then, when she sees the brook, is when Lily should get off.

But Stogie sees the brook before Lily does. He

swishes his long tail and starts trotting. Beware trots after him.

"No," Lily says. "Whoa!" But Beware wants to be with Stogie. She pulls against the bit. The pony did that all the time, but Beware hardly ever does.

"Beware!" Lily says sternly. She sits firmly in the saddle, and she makes Beware stop. "That's better," she says, and she gets off.

Is this the right thing to do? It feels strange to take Beware's bridle off while her saddle is still on, while she's still a half mile from home. Lily looks ahead to Stogie, drinking from the brook. Now she'll have two loose horses.

But that's what Gramp said to do. "All right," Lily mutters, and she slides the bridle over Beware's ears.

Beware shakes herself, so hard the stirrups thump against her sides. She trots to the brook and pushes in beside Stogie. He lifts his head, and they touch noses.

Lily waits for the squeal, the strike, the kick. But Stogie just sighs. He pushes his head into the curve of Beware's neck and rubs his face gently up and down, the way Beware sometimes rubs against Lily.

Beware lets Stogie rub for a minute. She mumbles her lips along his neck. Then she pulls away and puts her head down to drink.

Stogie starts to drink again, too. With every big swallow his ears twitch back and his throat makes a sound—*gunk! gunk! gunk!*

But Stogie *can't* drink any more! He's too hot, and he hasn't drunk for a long time. Too much cold water will make him sick.

Lily hurries down to where Beware stands drinking. She reaches across Beware's neck. Stogie is so close Lily can push him with her hand. "Stop!"

Stogie looks at her. He steps farther into the brook and puts his head down again.

Lily looks at the whip and the bridle in her hands. She could hit Stogie or throw the bridle at him. She could scare him out of the brook, and that would save him from getting sick.

But it seems wrong to scare Stogie now. Lily just touched him. Twice.

Stogie swallows again, and Lily lets the whip fall. She steps into the brook, straight to Stogie's head, and loops the rope around his neck. "No, Stogie," she says, and she pulls his head up.

Water drips from Stogie's muzzle. Water flows around Lily's feet, so cold she can feel it through her boots. Stogie looks at her. He doesn't pull. He doesn't try to bite. He just waits for what will happen next.

Lily hardly dares to breathe. Very gently she lets the halter slide down her shoulder. She works it along her arm until her hand can reach it, moving slowly so she doesn't frighten Stogie. When she has the halter in her hands, Lily spreads it wide, and lifts it toward Stogie's nose.

Stogie tosses his head.

"No!" Lily says firmly. She reaches up more quickly this time. Stogie tosses his head again, but

Lily gets the halter on his nose. She slides it up over his ears, just as if he were any other horse. She snaps the throat strap shut, and she clips the lead rope into the ring.

Stogie bobs his head toward the water. He bumps against the rope in Lily's hand. "No," she tells him. "You can have more later."

Now what? The last time anybody led Stogie was when Gramp took him off the truck. Lily can remember how beautiful he looked, and how he pranced beside Gramp. He wasn't hard to lead, and when he was let loose, he didn't kick up his heels until he was far away from Gramp. But he never let Gramp close enough to touch him again.

Now Lily is standing in the middle of a brook, holding a rope that's clipped to Stogie's halter. She's half a mile from home. One of her boots has a leak, and cold water trickles under her toes. She'd like to get out, but when she takes the first step, what will Stogie do?

Behind Lily, Beware shakes herself. The saddle

leather squeaks. Beware walks calmly past Stogie and Lily, splashing through the brook and up the bank on the other side. At the top of the bank she starts to trot. In a second she's out of sight.

CHAPTER NINE

"Beware!" Lily calls. "Beware!"

Stogie calls, too. He screams after Beware, so loud and close that it hurts Lily's ear. His hooves splash in the brook. He's dragging Lily up the bank. For a second she feels her feet running in the air, not touching the ground.

Beware is across the field already. She has turned to look at them, but Lily knows she won't come back. Beware wants to go home.

Stogie wants to be with Beware. He's trotting,

pulling Lily forward so fast she almost falls. Lily digs in her heels and pulls back. She presses her shoulder against Stogie's shoulder. "Whoa!"

Stogie doesn't slow down. One hoof bangs down on Lily's foot, and off again, so quickly that it doesn't seem to hurt. But halfway across the field Lily begins to feel it. "Beware! Wait!"

Beware does wait, but when Stogie gets close, she turns again. She trots along the little trail through the pines. Her ears are pricked, and she carries her tail gaily.

Stogie trots too, and Lily has to run to keep up. He knocks her with his shoulder. He bangs her with his knee. He pulls her along, and Lily can feel her body getting ahead of her legs. She'll fall down, or she'll have to let go, and Stogie will be loose again.

"Stop!" Lily screams. Her voice comes thin and breathless. The dark trees blur past. She can't see. . . .

Yes, she can. Up ahead it's getting lighter. They're coming to the big hayfield. As soon as she reaches it, Beware will kick up her heels and start to gallop. Then Lily will have to let Stogie go.

I will not! The words are in Lily's head because she has no breath left. But they're strong just the same, strong with anger.

Lily looks ahead for the right kind of tree. Near the edge of the woods she sees one, a straight, sturdy young maple.

Closer. Closer. Beware bursts out into the hayfield and kicks up her heels. Stogie surges after, but at the same moment Lily steps off the path, to the other side of the tree.

The rope twangs hard against the trunk and slides across it as Stogie keeps going. Lily's hands are pulled toward the tree. That will hurt. She'll have to let go—

No. Lily lets go with one hand. She reaches around the tree and grabs the loose end of the rope. Now she has a loop around the tree and the free end tight in both hands. Stogie hits the end of the rope and snaps himself around to face Lily. The tree trunk bounces. Above their heads the leaves rustle and go still.

It all happened in a few seconds. Lily's heart still pounds from running. Her breath moves her like ocean waves moving a boat. Stogie's hot breath blows over her. Lily reaches around the tree and makes one more loop with the rope. There's not enough end left to tie, but there's enough to hold.

Stogie twists to look after Beware. He neighs and yanks the rope. Lily waits. Sometimes horses panic when they're tied, lean back and pull with all their strength. If Stogie does that, even the two loops won't hold him. Lily will let him go.

But Stogie has spent this whole day hitched to a tree. He bumps against the halter, tugs on the rope, and neighs. But he doesn't panic, and he doesn't pull hard. He seems to know that he is stuck again and that pulling won't help.

While Stogie listens for Beware, Lily hears the quiet. Home is just two fields away. What is happening there? Does Gran see Beware coming home with no bridle? Is Gramp there, and does he know where to come looking? How long will Lily have to wait?

The sun is setting. It will be dark in a while. "We'll stay here all night if we have to!" Lily tells Stogie. She shifts her weight off her aching foot.

Stogie seems to listen to Lily. Then he turns his head and neighs again, sending his voice as far as he can across the field and hill.

"Keep that up!" Lily says. "That's good!"

Time passes slowly. Stogie doesn't neigh as often. He looks tired and sorry for himself. Lily would like to pat him, but she doesn't dare take a hand off the rope. Stogie must not feel that the rope can loosen at all.

Sweat dries and prickles on Lily's face. Her nose itches. She leans close to the tree trunk and rubs it against the bark.

Has she been standing here a long time? It seems

so, but the sun has still not set when Stogie suddenly turns his head toward home and pricks his ears. After a moment he neighs loudly. A second later a squashed old green hat rises over the crest of the hill. Then the pointed red ears of a horse: It's Gramp! He's riding! Gramp hardly ever rides. He says he's too old and fat, and he likes to keep both feet on the ground. Now he is trotting fast toward Lily, squinting under his hat brim. Mom canters over the hill behind him on Beware.

Lily can't wave, and she doesn't want to shout. Gramp rides up close and looks hard at her. "All right, Lily?"

Lily nods.

Gramp's whole body relaxes. He turns as Mom rides up. "All right, Barb," he says. "She's all right."

Mom's face slowly turns from white to pink. Lily looks away. They were scared, but she couldn't help it. There was nothing else she could do.

Now Gramp looks at Stogie, and the rope, and

the tree trunk. A smile begins on his face. "Where'd you find him?"

"His halter was caught on a branch, on the trail below where you cut wood."

"I'd forgotten all about that trail," Mom says.

"How'd you get him loose?" Gramp asks.

"I—" Lily stops. All at once she feels like crying, and she doesn't feel at all like telling her story.

"Pop," Mom says.

Gramp says, "I know. I'm just talkin' while I figure out what to do next." He climbs down stiffly from the red horse. "Will he let me come up to him, Lil? I don't want to scare him and make him fight. What do you think?"

Lily considers. Stogie has never once acted the way she was afraid he would act. He didn't strike at her when she stepped in front of him. He didn't run when she pushed him. He let her put his halter back on.

"I think he'll be okay," she says.

Gramp hands the red horse's reins to Mom. Slowly he saunters toward Stogie.

Stogie is looking past Gramp, at the other horses. But as Gramp get close, he starts to back. Gramp stops.

"Bring Beware up close," Lily says. "He likes Beware."

Mom dismounts and gives Beware to Gramp. That's when Lily notices that Beware is wearing only a halter, with two lead ropes clipped to it for reins. Mom was cantering her like that!

"Gran must be worried," Lily says.

"If we're not back in half an hour, she'll have Fire and Rescue out looking for us," Gramp says. "I wasn't too tore up"—Mom makes a little sound—"because I saw Beware's bridle was off. Figured you'd done just what I told you."

As he talks, Gramp leads Beware up to Stogie. While the horses sniff noses, Gramp reaches under Stogie's chin and takes hold of the rope with both hands.

"You can let go now," he says.

Lily's hands stick to the rope a little. They are sweaty, and they hurt. Lily stretches them and rubs her palms. She has rope burns. She didn't know that before.

"Take Beware," Gramp says. Lily moves out from behind the tree and takes Beware's lead ropes. Beware turns to sniff Lily's hands, and Stogie sniffs, too.

Then he seems to notice Gramp. His ears flick back—not in a mean way, but in a thinking way. Gramp and Lily stand very still.

After a moment Stogie sighs. His neck lowers, and his ears droop a little.

"He must have had himself a heck of a day!" Gramp says. "Now, Lily, mount up and ride as close to him as you can. We'll just stroll on home."

It sounds easy, and it is easy. With Beware right beside him, Stogie doesn't hurry anymore. He walks with his head low. He lets Gramp put a hand on his neck and rub him, and he even leans into Gramp's hand.

"He likes it," Lily says.

"He's going to find a lot to like about me," Gramp says.

Mom rides close to Lily. "Give me your hand."

Lily reaches out, and Mom squeezes her hand tight. "Ow!"

"Sorry."

They come over the last hill, and there is the barn and the big pasture with the cow and horses. The pony whinnies for Beware.

Up on the lawn stands Gran, straight and still. Lily waves, just once, so she doesn't scare Stogie. Gran lifts her hand high over her head and waves back. Then she turns toward the house.

"You rode Beware without a bridle," Lily says to Mom. "You cantered!"

"Yup, I was glad to see that," Gramp says. "Need somebody to ride this horse for me!" He glances up at Mom under the brim of his hat. Gramp is always trying to get Mom to ride more. He thinks she works too hard.

"Linwood Griffin!" Mom says.

"Now, Barb. This horse means an awful lot to me. I'd ask Lily, but Lily's got Beware."

"Ride him yourself!"

"I'm too old and fat for a horse like this," Gramp says. But Lily sees his eyes go faraway and sparkly. Gramp is imagining it. And maybe it could happen. Here they are, leading Stogie down the slope to the barn, after two whole years.

Lily smooths Beware's black mane with her fingers.

Anything could happen.